THESE DETESTABLE SLAVES OF THE DEVILL:

A Concise Guide to Witchcraft in Colonial Virginia

By

Carson O. Hudson Jr.

ISBN 0-7414-0859-7

Published by:

INFI∞ITY
PUBLISHING.COM

Infinity Publishing.com
519 West Lancaster Avenue
Haverford, PA 19041-1413
Info@buybooksontheweb.com
www.buybooksontheweb.com
Toll-free (877) BUY BOOK
Local Phone (610) 520-2500
Fax (610) 519-0261

Printed in the United States of America

Printed on Recycled Paper

Published November, 2001

Dedication

To the memory of Katherine Grady.

Hanged as a witch, off the coast of Virginia, 1654.

Acknowledgements

In researching and writing about witchcraft in colonial Virginia, one feels much like the freeholders that comprised the juries of the county courts of the period. First, each instance of witchcraft must be discovered and investigated. Then, research needs to be conducted into the facts of each case. Finally, one must obtain opinions and make decisions regarding what may have actually happened in each case and what is legend or local Virginia folklore of the last three hundred-plus years.

It would have been impossible to complete my investigations without the help of a number of friends and associates at the Colonial Williamsburg Foundation. They offered assistance, guidance, and advice.

Especially valued were the opinions and suggestions of Jeremy Fried and Tom Hay, both fine historians of colonial Virginia law. Abigail Schumann shared her knowledge of seventeenth century Virginia. Lou Powers and Kevin Kelly of Colonial Williamsburg's research department readily answered my often-strange questions. Gail Greve, Del Moore, and Juleigh Clark, along with the rest of the staff of the Rockefeller Library, were of great assistance in locating obscure books and documents.

The helpful staff of the Virginia State Library guided me through an untold number of county records.

Anna Holloway, of the Mariner's Museum in Newport News, Virginia, reviewed my notes and gave me valuable feedback.

As always, my good friend Anne Marie Millar gave me constructive criticism. Finally, Valli Anne Trusler suffered through my many requests for her opinion.

To all those who helped, I give my thanks.

Carson Hudson

CONTENTS

Introduction

On April 26, 1607, three small ships, the *Susan Constant*, the *Godspeed*, and the *Discovery*, arrived off the coast of Virginia. They brought with them 104 men and boys who would construct a wooden palisade at a spot they called Jamestown, named for their King, James I. Thus, the first permanent English settlement in North America was established.

The settlers that arrived on that spring day brought with them their thoughts of home and their beliefs and values. Among their beliefs was the conviction that witches were alive and thriving in the world.

The seventeenth century was an age when witches and demons, alchemists and sorcerers, sea monsters and fanciful creatures, were accepted by Englishmen, regardless of their social or intellectual station in life. A brief investigation of the literature and plays of their acquaintance confirms these beliefs. It is illustrated in such pieces as Christopher Marlowe's *Doctor Faustus* and William Shakespeare's *Macbeth*, *Midsummer Night's Dream*, and *The Tempest*.

Virginia, with its dark forests and strange native inhabitants, must have seemed quite frightening indeed. King James himself had written that the Devil's handiwork was "thought to be most common in such wilde partes of the world." It was there that "the Devill findes greatest ignorance and barbaritie." For at least the next hundred years, Virginians would be on the lookout for the Devil and his followers.

Over the years, much has been written about colonial witchcraft, primarily about the infamous Salem, Massachusetts witch trials. When one thinks of a witch trial in colonial America, the image of a narrow-minded Puritan judge self-righteously presiding over a predisposed court, sentencing dozens of innocent women to death, comes to mind. In point of fact, although there was a fear of witchcraft in every British colony of the seventeenth and early eighteenth centuries, except for the aberration of the Salem trials, no widespread witch-hunts occurred in England's North American colonies.

That, however, does not mean that there were no witchcraft proceedings in Virginia. Throughout the period, there were a number of examinations into the accusation of witchcraft and sorcery. Unfortunately, because of wars and neglect, many of Virginia's colonial documents and records have been lost. What survives is an incomplete record at best. Over time, stories of alleged witchcraft have been embellished with folklore and legend to produce tales that are amusing for the readers of ghost stories and mysteries, but which have little or no historical truth.

This volume is intended to be a quick and easy reference to the surviving records and known facts about the time when early Virginians imagined Satan to be walking amongst them.

Part the First:

The Beliefs
Being a brief description of some of the witchcraft beliefs of the early inhabitants of colonial Virginia.

Today we tend to associate witches with the familiar images of black pointed hats, cats, and old hags flying on brooms. Except for Halloween and the occasional movie or television program, most people don't often think about witches. It is hard to imagine a time when the idea of witches as servants of the Devil was a seriously accepted belief.

Yet, to colonial Virginians, witchcraft was real. It was mentioned in the Bible and educated men wrote volumes of literature concerning the activities and traits of supposed witches.

According to common opinion, no one was born a witch. They were ordinary human beings who had forsaken baptism and sworn allegiance to Satan. They had made a pact with the Devil, signed their name in his black book, and received his mark upon their bodies. In return, they acquired powers to cause mischief and harm. They used curses and spells to ruin crops, spoil milk, cause storms, and sicken livestock. They delighted in plaguing, crippling, or even killing innocent men, women, and children.

There were certain generally accepted beliefs and superstitions related to the lives and activities of witches. Although there were always some persons who did not adhere to various viewpoints or tales, it is safe to say that these beliefs went back to the British Isles and were familiar among the early settlers in Vir-

1

ginia, who brought these notions with them as surely as they brought the clothes on their backs.

Devil's Marks

A common popular belief was that when a witch made a pact with the Devil, he would mark that person with a hot iron or his tongue, thereby leaving "the Devil's mark." The marks were in secret places such as armpits or "private partes." They were considered to be insensitive to pain and, sometimes, unable to bleed. An examination for witchcraft would often include a search for such marks and every mole, birthmark, blemish, and scar would come under close scrutiny and, very possibly, pricking with a pin. Satan, purportedly, would also give each witch an extra teat or nipple, so that a familiar, or demon servant, could nourish themselves on a witch's blood. This was known as the "witch's mark" or witch's teat. The term witch's mark was often used interchangeably with Devil's mark. In 1705 John Bell, a Scottish minister, wrote a discourse in which he described his experience with a witch's mark:

This mark is sometimes like a little Teate; sometimes like a blewish spot: and I myself have seen it in the body of a confessing Witch like a little powder mark of a blea colour, somewhat hard, and withal insensible, so as it did not bleed when I pricked it.

"Devil's marks" were considered to have no feeling. Therefore, an examiner could detect a witch by sticking a suspicious mark with a pin or pricker. The use of torture to discover a witch or gain a confession was technically illegal in England and, accordingly, in

Virginia. Pricking, however, was considered not to be torture, but a test.

Virginia courts were known to have ordered examinations for Devil's or witch's marks on several occasions. Usually the magistrates would take care to assure that any jury formed to search for such marks would have some knowledge of the body, so that normal and natural body marks would not be mistaken for a pact with the Devil. In the 1706 case of Grace Sherwood, for example, the Princess Anne County Court prescribed that the jury impaneled to search her person was to be composed of "ancient and knowing women." The juries were to be of the same sex as the person accused and in the case of a woman, to have at least one midwife present rather than a doctor.

A jury of women impaneled to examine the body of a suspected witch was a jury of inquiry, not a trial jury. They were a fact-finding body, comparable to a coroner's jury, but their findings did not possess the dignity of a verdict.

Familiar

A familiar was a demon servant of a supposed witch that would assist in carrying out spells, bewitchments, and mischief.

There was disagreement during the colonial period regarding how a witch actually obtained a familiar. Some believed that familiars were demons given to a new witch by the Devil when they sold their souls. Others held that familiars were the product of a magical spell and that they received their power from the witch and not the Devil.

Also known as a familiar spirit or imp, these familiars would usually assume the shape of a small animal, such as cats, dogs, toads, owls or mice. Still another notion held that these familiars were otherwise normal animals that had been bewitched. Since any animal or even insect could be a familiar it was consequently quite easy for an examining authority to find some household pet or vermin that could be considered in league with an accused witch.

It was also believed that the familiars craved blood as payment for their services. Witches would reward them with their own blood by suckling a familiar with a witch's teat or mark. Most treatises on the subject would list both a witch's mark and a familiar as a proof of witchcraft.

Hag Riding

All witches, supposedly, possessed the ability to fly from place to place. This survives to the present day with the image of a witch riding upon a broom. In seventeenth century England, however, a witch might use a horse or other farm animal that had been bewitched for flight. If a "mare" was unavailable, a witch could climb on the back of a human who was then made to gallop about at the witch's command. Since such activities always took place at night, they were called "night-mares."

Victims of such a nightmarish excursion often described feelings of falling, great weights upon the body, or even suffocation. Such a victim was said to have been "ridden" or "hag ridden." Today, such symptoms are identified as a medical condition known as sleep paralysis. Early Virginians seemed to have been afflicted by hag riding, as it is mentioned in several witchcraft accusations throughout the colonial period.

Horseshoes

A widespread superstition of the colonial period that has survived into the present day is the belief that horseshoes are good luck amulets and ward off evil.

Englishmen of the seventeenth century considered a horseshoe to be a powerful talisman. If nailed over a door or window, they could supposedly prevent a witch from entering a dwelling. If placed in a chimney, they prevented witches from flying in. When nailed to a bedstead, they prevented bewitchments and nightmares. They could even be nailed to the mast of a vessel to keep a ship from harm.

To protect against witchcraft, the horseshoe would be positioned with the ends pointed down. If the ends were pointed up, the horseshoe then became a good luck charm.

There is direct evidence that the belief in a horseshoe's power was present in colonial Virginia and used as a test against a suspected witch in Northumberland County in 1671.

Puppets

Puppets (or poppets) were dolls, believed to have been made in the image of a person who was the object of a spell or curse. They could be made out of wood, wax, or dough, and included small bits of clothing, locks of hair, or nail clippings of the victim.

Supposedly, since the puppet was bound to a particular person through magic by the use of a personal item, they would contain the essence of that person. Actions against the puppet or figure, such as piercing with pins or nails, burning with a candle, or even hanging, would in some way affect the intended victim.

In his book *Demonologie*, written in 1597, King James VI of Scotland (later King James I of England) detailed how witches would cause harm to their victims:

To some others at these times he (the Devil) teacheth how to make pictures of wax or clay. That by the roasting thereof, the persons that they beare the name of, may be continually melted or dried away by continual sickness.

Early Virginians were familiar with, and believed in, a witch's use of puppets. In both the 1675 case of Joan Jenkins and the 1706 case of Grace Sherwood, county courts ordered that their houses be searched for "Images." Dalton's *Country Justice*, which was used as a legal reference by Virginia courts, reiterated King James' warnings:

They have often Pictures of Clay or Wax (like a Man, etc., made of such as they would bewitch) found in their House, or which they roast, or bury in the Earth, that as the Picture consumes, so may the parties bewitched consume.

Sea Storms

A commonly held belief of colonial Virginians was that a witch had the power to create a storm at sea and control the wind and rain.

At least three women were executed for being witches aboard ships that were involved in violent storms in or near Virginia waters. It is interesting to note, however, that it was the captain and crew of the vessels that executed, or lynched, those unfortunate women, rather than the proper legal authorities.

Nevertheless, even the learned among Virginia's gentry believed in the power of witches to cause or prevent a sea storm. A letter of 1735 from William Byrd II to a London Merchant stated, "I am glad to hear your ship the Williamsburg got home well, and that Crane (the captain) agreed with a witch at Hampton for a fair wind all the way."

Swimming

According to some authorities of the colonial period, a witch would be repelled by water because they had thrown off the waters of baptism. Therefore, a suspected witch could be discovered if she were placed into a body of water. King James I, an advocate of the test, explained what would happen:

It is a certain rule Witches deny their Baptism when they make Covenant with the Devill, water being the sole element thereof, and when they are heaved into the water it refuseth to receive them but suffers them to float.

Therefore, if an accused witch had made a pact with Satan, she would float on the water; if innocent, she would sink.

The test dated back to the Babylonian Code of Hammurabi (before the practice of baptism) and continued to be used into the 19th century. In the test, which was sometimes called ducking, the accused would be stripped down and bound, hands to feet. Sometimes the victim would be put into a porous bag or tied in a bed sheet. Ropes would be tied around their waist and they would be thrown into a nearby lake or pond. If they sank and proved their innocence, then the ropes would be used to save the accused from drowning by pulling them from the water.

The only known witchcraft case in which the test was used in Virginia was during the examination of Grace Sherwood of Princess Anne County in 1706. Located in the present-day City of Virginia Beach is a street still named "Witchduck Road," near the spot where Grace was "tried by water."

Transformation

In order to spread mischief without being detected, or to escape pursuit, witches were believed to have the ability to transform themselves into an animal's shape or form. Although this is closely related to the belief of lycanthropy or were-wolves, it was thought that witches usually changed into more discrete animals like dogs or cats.

In at least one Virginia case in Princess Anne County in 1698, mention of a supposed transformation was made. A woman of the county, Elizabeth Barnes, declared that Grace Sherwood had visited her house and left by disappearing out the keyhole "like a black Catt."

Witch Bottles

In seventeenth century England, many people used witch bottles to counteract the presence of a witch or their spells. These witch bottles were ceramic or glass flasks in which urine, nail clippings, hair, pins, etc. would be placed. According to common belief, the bottle symbolized the witch's bladder and the enclosed objects would cause the witch to experience agonizing pain. If such a container was buried under a door, window, or hearth, a witch would be unable to enter a household to cause mischief.

Many of these witch bottles have been recovered archaeologically at sites in England dating from the seventeenth century through the late nineteenth century. Similar finds have been unearthed in Virginia, Maryland, and Pennsylvania. In 1979, archaeologists working on a seventeenth century house site near Great Neck Point in Virginia Beach discovered an inverted glass vial, suspected to be a witch bottle, filled with brass pins in a yellowish liquid.

Another known protection was a "witch box." Popular in sixteenth and seventeenth century England, they were usually wooden boxes with a glass front. Inside would be placed herbs, pins, bones, and other miscellany over which a magic spell was cast, in the hopes of discouraging witches and evil.

A curious related custom was the use of shoes, concealed in fireplaces and chimneys of a house, assumed to ward off witches and evil. It is possible, however, these shoe concealments were instead meant to be more of a good luck tradition than witchcraft deterrent. Discoveries of "shoe concealment" have been made during the renovation and restoration of various colonial buildings in Virginia.

Part the Second:

The Law

Consisting of the more notable legal statutes and opinions regarding witchcraft as they affected the Colony of Virginia.

Colonial Virginians had a four-tiered system of courts. First, there were single magistrates, or justices of the peace, who could act summarily, as in small claims cases. Next, there were the local county courts, which consisted of at least four justices of the peace (a quorum) sitting on the bench on established court days. These courts of record heard matters of property, settled simple disputes, and held examining courts.

Felony matters were serious enough that the punishment was death by hanging. Throughout the seventeenth century, there was only one court in Virginia that could hear such cases, the General Court. Everyone accused of a felonious crime was tried by this court, which was presided over by the Governor and his council. By the eighteenth century, felonious cases involving slaves could be held at the county level. Until 1699, the General Court was located at Jamestown, at which time it was moved with the capital to Williamsburg.

Finally, the highest level of the legal system was the King, but cases from Virginia rarely reached that point.

Accusations of witchcraft would normally originate in a county court. If the county justices found no evidence, or if the supposed witchcraft was not considered serious enough, the matter would end there with a simple judgment. On the other hand, if the evidence

10

warranted, or if the charge was of a felonious nature, then the accused would be sent to the capital, to the General Court, under the care of a sheriff. There the King's (or Queen's) Attorney would represent the Crown, as the accused attempted to disprove the allegations against themselves.

As in all felony cases, the testimony of two witnesses was required for a conviction. This presented a problem in witchcraft cases in that the relationship between the devil and a witch was, by definition, hidden or invisible. A witness would rarely, if ever, observe an accused witch actually performing an act of witchcraft. Instead, evidence would consist of the effects of a witch's power, apparitions, familiars and specters, or "spectral evidence."

Legally speaking, Virginia Courts were following English law and statutes. In practice, English law and statutes were interpreted as needed and became "Virginia Law."

The Witchcraft Acts

The English Parliament passed its first statute against witchcraft during the reign of King Henry VIII, in 1542. Before that time, witchcraft accusations in England had been handled primarily by ecclesiastical courts. The Act of 1542 was repealed only five years later.

During the reign of Queen Elizabeth I, a second act was passed, the Act of 1563. Influenced by the witchcraft manias occurring on the Continent, the act stated:

If any person or persons after the saide first day of June shall use, practise or exercise Witchcraft, enchantment or sorcery, whereby any person shall hap-

pen to be killed or destroyed, they shall suffer pains of death as Felon or Felons.

The third major witchcraft Act, and the one that was to affect the early Virginia settlers, was the Act of 1604 or the Witchcraft Statute of James I.

Statute of James I

In 1589, the intended bride of King James VI of Scotland, Princess Anne of Denmark, was prevented from crossing over the North Sea by a terrible storm. Personally embarking to retrieve her, the King encountered an even more violent storm that caused the delay of the couple in returning to Scotland. It was rumored that Danish witches caused the King's difficulties.

In the aftermath of several trials and amidst the confessions of suspected witches in both Denmark and Scotland, King James became convinced that the Devil was out to destroy him. According to one confession, there had been a great assembly of witches, at which Satan had declared, "James was the greatest enemy he ever had." The King began a serious study of witchcraft and personally examined some accused witches. A scholarly man, he published a philosophical treatise on the subject titled *Demonology*, in 1597.

Because of his staunch beliefs, when he came to the throne of England in 1603 as James I, he caused to be enacted a new witchcraft statute. Adopted by Parliament in 1604, the Witchcraft Statute of James I created a wider interpretation of the activities of supposed witches and prescribed harsher punishments for those convicted.

The Act divided the crime into two "degrees." Witchcraft of the first degree included causing death or destruction through the conjuration of an evil spirit or the use of charms or sorcery. Punishment for such a conviction was death by hanging. Second degree or "petit" witchcraft was defined as offering to find buried treasure, locate stolen goods, or using potions or charms to provoke "unlawful love." For the first offence of "petit" witchcraft, punishment was a year's imprisonment, and being placed in a public pillory every three months, where the convicted would openly confess their offences. A second conviction would bring a death sentence.

When the first colonists arrived at Jamestown in 1607, they were subject to British statutes and consequently the Witchcraft Statute of James I was applied to such matters appearing before Virginia courts.

The Country Justice

In 1618, Michael Dalton published a summary of English law entitled *The Country Justice*. Since there was no requirement to posses a legal education to become a justice of the peace, Dalton's work was intended as a handbook for those who sat on the bench. It was well received in Virginia and was used extensively by county court clerks and justices of the peace. *The Country Justice* was found in the law libraries of many Virginians throughout the entire colonial period.

In his book, Dalton placed the subject of witchcraft under the heading of "Conjuration," which was inserted in "Felonies by Statute." He listed nine types of activities that were punishable under the law:

> 1. *Conjuration, or Invocation of any evill spirit, for any intent, &c. or to be counselling or aiding thereto, is felony, without benefit of Clergy. See Exod.22.18.*

13

2. *To consult, covenant with, entertaine, imploy, feede, or reward any evill spirit, is felonie in such offenders, their aydors, and counsellers.*

3. *To take up any dead body, or any part thereof to be imploied or used in any maner of witchcraft, is felony in such offenders, their aydors, and counsellers.*

4. *Also to use or practice Witchcraft, Inchantment, Charme, or Sorcery, whereby any person shall be killed, pined, or lamed in any part of their body, or to be counseling or aiding thereto, is felony.*

5. *Also the second time to practice Witchcraft, &c. thereby to declare where any treasure may be found.*

6. *Or where any goods lost, or stollen, may be found.*

7. *Or wherby any cattel or goods shalbe destroied or impaired.*

8. *Or to the intent to provoke any person to love.*

9. *Or to the intent to hurt any person in their body, though it be not effected. All these are felony, the second offence; and without benefit of Clergy.*

Dalton went on to provide a guide for gathering evidence of witchcraft by referring to an English Assize case of 1612:

Now against these witches the Justices of peace may not alwaies expect direct evidence, seeing all their works are the works of darknesse, and no witnesses present with them to accuse them; And therefore their better discovery, I thought good here to insert certain observations out of the book of discovery of the witches that were arraigned at Lancaster, Ann. Dom. 1612, before Sir James Altham, and Sir Edw. Beverly Judges of Assise there.

1. *These Witches have ordinarily a familiar, or spirit, which appeareth to them.*

2. *Their said familiar hath some bigg or little teat upon their body and in some secret place, where he sucketh them.*

3. *They have often pictures of Clay, or Waxe (like a man, &c.) found in their house.*

4. *If the dead body bleed, upon the Witches touching it.*

5. *The testimony of the person hurt, upon his death.*

6. *The examination and confession of the children, or servants of the Witch.*

7. *Their owne voluntarie confession, which exceedes all other evidence.*

Dalton's *Country Justice* was not superseded until 1755 in England. However, in 1736, a Virginia justice named Webb published an updated handbook, *The Office and Authority of a Justice of Peace.*

The Act of 1736

The Witchcraft Statute of James I was repealed in 1736, after minimal opposition, and replaced by the Act of 1736. The new statute removed witchcraft as a felony, but retained the punishment of a year's imprisonment and public repentance for "persons pretending to use witchcraft, tell fortunes or discover stolen goods by skill in the occult sciences." The Act of 1736 remained in force until 1951.

The Office And Authority of A Justice of Peace

In 1736 George Webb, a justice of the peace in New Kent County, published *The Office And Authority of A Justice of Peace.* Printed in Williamsburg, it was known within the colony as "Webb's *Justice.*" Webb's book was a compilation and summary of "the Common and Statute Laws of England, and Acts of Assembly, now in Force: And adapted to the Constitution and Practice of Virginia." The book was intended to replace Dalton's *The Country Justice,* of 1618.

On the subject of witchcraft, Webb wrote:

The Existence of Witches, or Persons of either Sex, who have real Correspondence and familiar Conversation with Evil Spirits, has been a Subject of controversy among learned Men; And latter Ages have produced very few Instances of Convictions of Witchcraft: But nevertheless, 'tis a Capital Offence...

16

Not yet reflecting the new Witchcraft Act of 1736, Webb's book went on to list the actual offenses of witchcraft, noting that certain of these crimes were felonies, while others were merely punishable by one year's imprisonment without bail. The convicted witch had to stand in the pillory every quarter of that year and publicly confess their offense. He concluded with the advice that:

Information of Witchcraft ought not to be received by Justices of Peace, nor Prosecution awarded thereupon, without strong and apparent Cause, proved by sufficient Witnesses, upon Oath: If Process is found necessary, the Proceedings must be as in other Capital Offences.

Despite the decriminalization of witchcraft and the decline in prosecutions after 1736, many educated and respected people remained steadfast in their beliefs. In 1775, the noted legal expert William Blackstone wrote:

To deny the possibility, nay, actual existence of witchcraft and sorcery, is at once flatly to contradict the revealed word of God, in various passages both of the old and new testament: and the thing itself is a truth to which every nation in the world hath in its turn borne testimony, either by examples seemingly well attested, or by prohibitory laws; which at least suppose the possibility of a commerce with evil spirits.

Benefit of Clergy
In colonial Virginia, the General Court at Jamestown, and later in Williamsburg, was the only tribunal in the colony that could impose a death sen-

tence against a free defendant. A felon convicted by the General Court and sentenced to execution could, in some cases, escape his fate by pleading "benefit of clergy."

Dating from the Middle Ages, this legal privilege of escape could be granted by the court to any prisoner who could demonstrate an ability to read a passage from the Bible. In England, the 51st Psalm was commonly used. Upon successfully reading the prescribed passage, a condemned felon would be branded and then released. A repeat criminal could claim the benefit of clergy only once.

Before 1732, the privilege was normally only extended to white males. After that date, women, Negroes, mulattoes, and Indians were legally allowed to ask for consideration, although there are instances of it being allowed in cases prior to 1732.

The benefit of clergy could not be given to a felon whose crime was willful murder, rape, treason, arson, horse stealing, burglary, or robbery. Witchcraft was also considered a crime "without benefit of clergy."

Part the Third:

The Experts
Being a Brief description of what the noted authorities on witchcraft had to say.

The existence of witches was not doubted by the average Englishman, and hence the average Virginian, in the seventeenth and early eighteenth century. What counted as evidence of witchcraft, however, was a matter of debate. Since the charge of witchcraft could bring a sentence of death, there was a great concern that no mistakes be made in the true discovery of a witch.

Fortunately for the largely untrained justices who sat in the courts of colonial Virginia, there was a wealth of reference material available regarding proper proof. For centuries, learned scholars had written and discussed the correct way to discover witches. In response, there were also critics of "witch finding." The gentleman justices of Virginia could consult a number of authorities.

Malleus Maleficarum
Written by two Dominican friars, Heinrich Kramer and Jakob Sprenger, *Malleus Maleficarum* (*The Hammer of Witches*) was one of the earliest and most influential books ever published on witchcraft. Published in Latin in 1486, it became the definitive work on how to discover and punish witches. Although popular throughout Europe, the first English translation was not printed until 1584. Records indicate that it was consulted and referred to, but its impact in Anglican English courts was weakened by the fact that

it was a Catholic treatise. The book was known and available to educated Virginians in the colonial period.

Discovery of Witchcraft

In his book, *The Discovery of Witchcraft*, published in England in 1584, Reginald Scot warned that learned men and justices of the peace should exercise common sense and caution during witchcraft examinations. He detailed how mountebanks and conjurors could fool people with simple tricks and that many of the so-called witches were actually only harmless old women. King James VI of Scotland countered Scot's assertions in his own book, *Demonologie*, published in 1597. When he later became King of England in 1603, he ordered that all copies of Scot's book were to be burned. The work survived, however, as a testament against the persecutions of the time.

Demonologie

King James VI published a book entitled *Demonologie* in 1597, which he had personally handwritten as a refutation of Reginald Scot's *The Discovery of Witchcraft*. In the Preface he referred to witches as "these detestable slaves of the Devill."

Written as a fictional, philosophical dialog between two scholars, *Demonolgie* put forth the creed that witches and witchcraft truly existed and that authorities should hunt and prosecute all the earthly followers of Satan. In the chapter on "the tryall and punishment of witches," two scholars, Philomathes and Epistemon, discuss the proper punishment for witchcraft:

PHILOMATHES: Then to make an ende of our conference, since I see it drawes late, what forme of punishment thinke ye merites these Magicians and Witches? for I see that ye account them to be all alike guiltie?

EPISTEMON: They ought to be put to death according to the Law of God, the civill and imperial law, and municipall law of all Christian nations.

PHILOMATHES: But what kinde of death, I pray you?

EPISTEMON: It is commonly used by fire, but that is an indifferent thing to be used in every cuntrie, according to the Law or custome thereof.

PHILOMATHES: But ought no sexe, age nor ranck to be exempted?

EPISTEMON: None at all (being so used by the lawful Magistrate) for it is the highest poynt of Idolatrie, wherein no exception is admitted by the law of God.

When he came to the throne of England in 1603, James' ideas on witchcraft and the supernatural came with him, just in time to influence the early English settlers in Virginia. Copies of *Demonolgie* are listed in the inventories of early Virginian's private libraries.

The King James Bible

In 1604, the same year that the witchcraft statutes of King James I were enacted, the King also authorized a commission of scholars to assemble a new and "uncorrupt" translation of the Bible. Published in 1611, the new *King James Bible* became the accepted Holy Writ for the Church of England. Colonial Virginians embraced it along with the *Book of Common Prayer* as they attended their Parish Churches.

Two verses in particular were used as proof of God's disapproval of witches:

> *Exodus 22:18 Thou shall not suffer a witch to live.*

> *Deuteronomy 18:10 There shall not be found among you any one that maketh his son or his daughter to pass through fire, or that useth divination, or an observer of times, or an enchanter, or a witch.*

Authorities in colonial Virginia were never as rabid in their prosecution of accused witches as were their counterparts in puritanical Massachusetts. The historical records suggest very little ecclesiastical influence in the surviving cases.

By the mid-eighteenth century, the religious revival known as the Great Awakening swept across the colonies and its effects were strongly felt in Virginia. "Enthusiastical" preachers such as Samuel Davies, William Robinson, and George Whitefield influenced many Virginians. Although most people's belief in witchcraft had fallen by the wayside before the Awakening occurred, there were holdouts among the Presbyterian and Methodist congregations in Virginia who still felt threatened by Satan's disciples. In 1768, John Wesley, the founder of Methodism, wrote:

The English in general, and indeed most of the men of learning in Europe, have given up all accounts of witches and apparitions as mere old wives fables. I am sorry for it, and I willingly take this opportunity of entering my solemn protest against this violent compliment which so many that believe in the Bible pay to those who do not believe it... the giving up of witchcraft is in effect giving up the Bible.

Discourse of the Damned Art of Witchcraft

The Puritan preacher William Perkins was a prolific writer who included among his works, sermons on witchcraft. His *Discourse of the Damned Art of Witchcraft*, published posthumously in 1608 and reprinted in a second edition in 1610, supported the ideas expressed by King James I in his book, *Demonologie*.

Perkins' views were a reasoned defense of the belief in witchcraft, although he did not ascribe to the use of superstitious tests, such as "ducking" or "swimming" an accused witch. He held that witchcraft accusations should be entered into with common sense and rational examination. If guilt was established, however, Perkins stated, "all Witches being thoroughly convicted by the Magistrate, ought according to the Law of Moses to be put to death."

In 1692, the Boston minister, Cotton Mather, listed a synopsis of "Mr. Perkins' way for the discovery of witches" in his book *The Wonders of the Invisible World*:

I.   *There are Presumptions, which do at least probably and conjecturally note one to be a Witch. These give occasion to examine, yet they are no sufficient Causes of Conviction.*

II.   *If any Man or Woman be notoriously defamed for a Witch this yields a strong
Suspition. Yet the Judge ought carefully
to look, that the Report be made by Men
of Honesty and Credit.*

III.   *If a Fellow-Witch, or Magician, give Testimony of any Person to be Witch; this
indeed is not sufficient for Condemna-
tion; but it is a fit Presumption to cause a
strait Examination.*

IV.   *If after Cursing there follow Death, or at
least some mischief: for Witches are wont
to practise their mischievous Facts by
Cursing and Banning: This also is a sufficient matter of Examination, tho' not of
Conviction.*

V.   *If after Enmity, Quarreling, or Threatening, a present mischief does follow; that
also is a great Presumption.*

VI.   *If the Party suspected be the Son or
Daughter, the man-servant or maid-
servant, the Familiar Friend, near Neighbor, or old Companion, of a known and
convicted witch; this may be likewise a
Presumption; for Witchcraft is an Art that
may be learned, and conveyed from man
to man.*

VII.   *Some add this for a Presumption: If the
Party suspected be found to have the*

Devil's mark; for it is commonly thought, when the Devil makes a Covenant with them, he alwaies leaves his mark behind them, whereby he knows them for his own: -- a mark whereof no evident Reason in Nature can be given.

VIII. *Lastly, If the party examined be Unconstant, or contrary to himself, in his deliberate Answers, it argueth a Guilty Conscience, which stops the freedom of Utterance. And yet there are causes of astonishment, which may befall the Good, as well as the Bad.*

IX. *But then there is a Conviction, discovering the Witch, which must proceed from just and sufficient proofs, and not from bare presumptions.*

X. *Scratching of the suspected party, and Recovery thereupon, with several other such weak Proofs; as also, the fleeting of the suspected Party, thrown upon the Water; these proofs are so far from being sufficient, that some of them are, after a sort, practices of witchcraft.*

XI. *The Testimony of some Wizzard, tho' offering to shew the Witches Face in a Glass: This, I grant, may be a good Presumption, to cause a strait Examination; but a sufficient Proof of Conviction it cannot be. If the Devil tell the Grand jury, that the person in question is a Witch, and offers withal to confirm the same by Oath, should the inquest receive his Oath or Accusation to condemn the man? Assuredly no. And yet, that is as much as the Testimony of another Wizzard, who only by the Devil's help reveals the Witch.*

XII. *If a man, being dangerously sick, and like to dye, upon Suspicion, will take it on his Death, that such a one hath bewitched him, it is an Allegation of the same nature, which may move the Judge to examine the Party, but it is of no moment for Conviction.*

XIII. *Among the sufficient means of Conviction, the first is, the free and voluntary Confession of the Crime, made by the party suspected and accused, after Examination. I say not, that a bare confession is sufficient, but a Confession after due Examination, taken upon pregnant presumptions. What needs now more witness or further Enquiry?*

XIV. *There is a second sufficient Conviction, by the Testimony of two Witnesses, of good and honest Report, avouching before the Magistrate, upon their own Knowledge, these two things: either that the party accused hath made a League with the Devil, or hath done some known practice of witchcraft. And, all Arguments that do necessarily prove either of these, being brought by two sufficient Witnesses, are of force fully to convince the party suspected.*

XV. *If it can be proved, that the party suspected hath called upon the Devil, or desired his Help, this is pregnant proof of a League formerly made between them.*

XVI. *If it can be proved, that the party hath entertained a Familiar Spirit, and had Conference with it, in the likeness of some visible Creatures; here is Evidence of witchcraft.*

XVII. *If the witnesses affirm upon Oath that the suspected person hath done any action or work which necessarily infers a Covenant made, as, that he hath used Enchantments, divined things before they come to pass, and that peremptorily, raised Tempests, caused the Form of a dead man to appear; it proveth sufficiently, that he or she is a Witch.*

Educated Virginians of the colonial period were familiar with Perkins' writings. In 1621, a three-volume set of Perkins' works had been dispatched to Virginia and eighteenth century inventories of private libraries reveal copies of his works. In 1744, for example, Colonel William Byrd II possessed a copy of Perkins' *Art of Witchcraft.*

The Displaying of Supposed Witchcraft

John Webster made an important contribution to the literature concerning witchcraft with his book, *The Displaying of Supposed Witchcraft*. With the coming of the Age of Reason, in which men began to look at the world around them with a scientific eye, Webster presented the idea that evidence of witchcraft should be subjected to the same scientific examination. Webster did not deny witchcraft. However, he felt that there was not the need to blame the Devil for every misfortune.

Published in London in 1677, Webster's book and views were known in Virginia, as is evidenced by a copy that resided in the chamber of Virginia's Council. Ralph Wormeley, president of the Council and acting governor of the colony for a short time in 1698, possessed his own volume of Webster's book. Upon his death in 1701, an inventory of Wormeley's library lists a copy of *The Displaying of Supposed Witchcraft*.

Saducimus Triumphatus

Even with the enlightened views of men such as John Webster, traditional views persisted. Joseph Glanville, the rector of Bath Abbey and a fellow of the Royal Society, wrote *Philosophical Considerations Touching Witches and Witchcraft* in 1666. Running through several editions, his work was republished posthumously in 1681 as *Saducimus Triumphatus; Or, Full and Plain Evidence Concerning Witches and Apparitions*.

Glanville felt that witches and witchcraft proved the existence of Satan and to deny them was close to denying the existence of God. He attempted to provide answers to objections of supernatural beliefs. In his

28

work he listed the attributes of witches, such as the ability to fly to remote places, transform into animals, and the raising of tempests or storms, all of which were common notions in colonial Virginia.

In 1733, a court-ordered inventory and appraisement of the personal estate of "Robert Beverly, Esq., deceased," of Spotsylvania County, lists a copy of Glanville's *Saducimus Triumphatus*.

Part the Fourth:

The Witches
Being a brief description of those poor, wretched souls accused of the crime of witchcraft in the Colony of Virginia and it's vicinage.

When the first English settlers arrived in Virginia and settled at Jamestown in 1607, they brought with them their belief in witchcraft and the supernatural. They were largely influenced by their King, an ardent believer who had published his views in his book, *Demonologie*.

It is not surprising that when these first settlers met the Native American inhabitants of Virginia, they immediately looked upon them as barbarians who worshiped idols and were under the influence of Satan. In 1612, Alexander Whitaker wrote that:

...in a march upp Nansemond River as our men passed by one of their Townes, there yssued out on the shoare a mad crewe dauncing like Anticks, or our Morris dancers before whom there were Quiokosite (or theire Priest) tossed smoke and flame out of a thinge like a censer. An Indian (by the name of Memchumps) amongst our men seeing this dance tould us that there would be very much raine presently and indeed there was a forthwith exceedinge thunder and lighteninge and much raine within 5 miles and so further of...All which things make me think that there be great witches amongst them and they very familiar with the divill.

Whitaker went on to say in his *Good Newes from Virginia*, that the Indian priests belonged to "a generation of vipers even of Sathans owne brood," and "are no other but such as our English Witches are."

In 1613, William Crashaw wrote of Virginia, that "Satan visibly and palpably raignes there, more than any other known place of the world." Master George Percy described the first Indians he encountered in Virginia as "so many wolves or Devils." Captain John Smith described even the chief of all the local tribes, the great Powhatan, as "more like a devill than a man."

Beginning in the mid 1620s, as the colony grew with new arrivals, the English settlers began to find disciples of the Devil in their own communities. The first recorded witchcraft inquiry in Virginia dates to 1626. From then until the early eighteenth century, the colony's surviving records indicate several witchcraft investigations, petitions, suits, and counter-suits. What follows is a chronological listing of those accused of witchcraft in colonial Virginia.

1626 – Joan Wright

On September 11, 1626, Joan Wright, the wife of Robert Wright of Surry County, was accused of witchcraft and brought before the General Court at Jamestown to be examined. The governor of the colony, Sir George Yeardley, presided as chief justice to determine if the accusations merited further legal proceedings. The court records are fragmentary, but provide an insight into witchcraft beliefs of the time. The first witness against Mrs. Wright was Lieutenant Giles Allington who stated:

That he harde Sargeant Booth saye that he was croste by a woman and for twelve months space he havinge very fayre game to shute at, yet he could never kill any thinge but this deponent cannot say that was good wiefe Wright.

Lieutenant Allington went on to say that he had spoken to Mrs. Wright, who was apparently a midwife, concerning the care of his wife during a pregnancy. Unfortunately, Joan Wright was left-handed, which was considered "different" or unlucky. The idea of a left-handed attendant at her child's birthing upset Allington's wife to such an extent that she made her husband retain the services of a second midwife. This apparently brought misfortune to Lieutenant Allington and his family. His statement continues:

...the next daye after his wiefe was delivered, the saide goodwiefe Wright went awaye from his house very much discontented, in regarde the other midwiefe had brought his wiefe to bedd, shortlie after this, this deponents wiefes brest grew dangerouslie sore of an Imposture and was a moneth or 5 weeks before she was recovered, Att which tyme This deponent him selfe fell sick and contynued the space of three weeks, And further sayeth that his childe after it was borne fell sick and soe contynued the space of two moneths, and afterwards recovered, And so did Contynue well for the space of a moneth, And afterwards fell into extreme payne the space of five weeks and so departed.

Under the law, this evidence, causing pain, sickness, and the death of a child, was more than enough to convict Mrs. Wright of a felony, if it could be proved.

The next witness, Rebecca Graye, told how Mrs. Wright had predicted that she would soon bury her husband. She went on to testify that a Mr. Felgate and Thomas Harris had also received similar warnings from Goodwife Wright concerning their respective spouses. According to the witnesses, Mrs. Wright seemed to be very good at foretelling death. Daniel Watkins, after being sworn by the court, recalled such an instance had occurred when Robert Thresher proposed to send a couple of hens to Elizabeth Arundle. Watkins stated that:

> *goodwiefe Wright being there in place, saide to Robert Thresher, "why do you keepe these henns heere tyed upp, The maide you meane to send them to will be dead before the henns come to her."*

Robert Thresher came forth to testify for himself and along with the statements of Elizabeth Gates, suggested that Mrs. Wright also had a tendency to cause property destruction:

> *Robert Thresher sworne and examined sayeth yt good wiefe Wright came to him and requested him to give her some plants, He answered yt when he had served his owne tourne, she should have some, so she went away and yt night all his plants were drowned...*
> *Elizabeth Gates sworne and examined sayeth yt Goodwiefe Wright came to Mr. Moores at Kickotan to buy some chickens, but he would sell her none, shortly after the chickens died, and after that the henn died, and this she affirmeth she had hearde from others.*

Mrs. Isabell Perry came forward to tell the court how Mrs. Wright had been causing trouble, even before she arrived in Surry County. Sometime before in

"Kickotan" in Elizabeth City County, Joan Wright had threatened a servant girl of Elizabeth Gates that if she didn't return some firewood that was stolen, that Goodwife Wright would make her "daunce starke naked."

Mrs. Perry went on to repeat gossip about how Goodwife Wright had been a witch as long ago as when she had lived in England at Hull.

In the next week, the court heard others who came forward offering supporting evidence. Finally, Joan Wright's husband was brought before the court, where he could only state that he had been married to her for sixteen years and knew nothing of her supposed crimes.

Here the records of the General Court's investigation end and there is no documentary evidence of an actual trial. Whatever the outcome, it is to be hoped that the court did not take any of the accusations seriously and that Mrs. Wright's neighbors left her alone.

1641 – Mrs. George Barker

In April of 1641, Jane Rookens apparently spoke in anger and called George Barker's wife a witch. It was Jane Rookens, however, that found herself in trouble. The General Court at Jamestown ruled against Mrs. Rookens in a slander suit. Jane's poor husband became the final victim. The court records state:

Wheras it appeareth to the court by several depositions that Jane Rookens hath abused and scandalized the wife of George Barker by calling her a witch which the said Rookens doth not remember but denyeth in open court and is sorry for the same offence with which the said Barker was very satisfied, the court hath therefore ordered that William Rookens husband of the said Jane forthwith pay unto the said Barker expenses and charges of court on this behalf sustained...

1654 – Katherine Grady

Katherine Grady has the unfortunate distinction of being the only known person who was executed for witchcraft in the colony of Virginia, although technically, she was not in the colony proper when she met her fate.

In the year 1654, Katherine was a passenger aboard a ship sailing for Virginia. Upon reaching the coast of the colony, the ship rode into a great storm. As it was a common belief that storms at sea were a favorite evil spell cast upon travelers by witches, the passengers and crew began to look about for a likely suspect. For whatever reason, poor Katherine Grady seems to have become the object of her fellow passengers fear and wrath. They convinced the ship's captain, a man named Bennett, that Katherine was the witch who was causing the tempest, to torment her companions. Captain Bennett took matters into his own hands and hanged Katherine, in an effort to end the storm.

Upon reaching port, the captain was called to appear before an admiralty court at Jamestown to answer for his actions. The court's findings are lost, but the fact remains that although there was no official trial or inquiry into the matter of Katherine Grady's supposed witchcraft, she became a colonial Virginia statistic only because Virginia was Captain Bennett's destination.

1656 – William Harding

Poor William Harding was living in Northumberland County on Virginia's Northern Neck when he was accused of witchcraft and sorcery. Reverend David

Lindsey of Wicomico Parish brought the accusations before a grand jury of 24 freeholders in November of 1656. The grand jury accepted several depositions against Harding and decided that some of the accusations were true. The county justices of the peace then deliberated over a proper punishment. Apparently, whatever Harding's witchcraft consisted of, it was not considered to be too life threatening because the justices ordered that:

>...the said Wm. Harding shall forthwith receave ten stripes upon his bare back and forever to be Banished from this County and that hee depart within the space of two moneths And also to pay all the charges of Court.

This constitutes one of only two known cases of a legal conviction for witchcraft in the Colony of Virginia.

1657– Barbara Wingbrough (Wingborough)

Barbara Wingbrough appeared before Governor Samuel Matthews and his council sitting as the General Court at Jamestown on December 1, 1657. There, she was "arragned as a witch but acquitted." Her accuser was Francis Doughty, who was perhaps influenced by religious zeal. He had been forced to leave England because of his Puritan beliefs and had settled initially in Massachusetts before coming to Virginia. By 1661, he had left Virginia and was residing in the neighboring colony of Maryland where he accused another woman of witchcraft. Regardless of his religious views, Doughty was described as being prone to "many vices and especially to drinking."

1659 – Mistress Robinson

The justices of the peace in early Colonial Virginia appear to have been more skeptical of charges of witchcraft than their New England counterparts. Although their belief in witchcraft and the supernatural was no different from any average Englishman of their time, they took a dim view of false accusations. In 1655, for example, the justices of Lower Norfolk County, meeting at "a private court" at the house of Edward Hall in Lynnhaven, ordered:

Whereas divrs dangerous & scandalous speeches have beene raised by some persons concerning sevrall women in this Countie termeing them to be Witches, whereby their reputacons have beene much impaired, and their lives brought in question (for avoydeing the like offence) It is by this Court ordered that what persons soer shall hereafter raise any such like scandal concerninge any partie whatsoever and shall not be able to pvr the same, both upon oath, and by sufficient witness, such person soe offending shall in the first place paie A thousand pounds of tob: and likewise be lyeable to further Censure of the Court.

In December of 1659, the court arraigned Ann Godby for "Slanders & scandals Cast upon Women under the notion of Witches." Several depositions were presented to the court telling how Mrs. Godby had slandered a Mistress Robinson of the county by calling her a witch. Ann's husband, Thomas, was also called forward as he was responsible under the law for his wife's actions. After hearing all the evidence the justices decided:

Whereas Ann Godby, the wife of Tho. Godby, hath contrary to an order of the court bearing the date of May 1655, concerning some slanders and scandals cast upon women under the notion of witches hat contemptuously acted in abusing and taking the good name and credit of Nico. Robinson's wife, terming her as a witch... It is therefore ordered that the sd Tho. Godby shall pay three hundred pounds of tobo & Caske fine for her Contempt of the menconed order, (being the first time) & also pay & defray the Cost of sute together with the Witnesses Charges at twenty Pounds tobo p day als exec.

Three years later, the House of Burgesses at Jamestown passed "An Act for Punishment of Scandalous Persons" which included a provision to protect husbands from the acts of their wives:

Whereas many babbling women slander and scandalize theire neighbors for which their poore husbands are often involved in chargeable and vexatious suits, and cast in great damnages, Be it therefore enacted by the authorities aforesaid that in actions of slander occasioned by the wife after judgment passed for the damnages, the woman shall be punished by ducking and if the slander be soe enormous as to be adjudged at greater damnages then five hundred pounds of tobacco then the woman to suffer a ducking for each five hundred pounds of tobacco adjudged against the husband if he refuse to pay the tobacco.

1659 – Elizabeth Richardson
Although not strictly a Virginia matter, the great-grandfather of George Washington was involved as a witness in a witchcraft matter in Maryland in 1659.

John Washington of Westmoreland County petitioned a Maryland court to investigate the matter of the execution of Elizabeth Richardson as a witch aboard a merchant ship in the Chesapeake Bay, off Virginia's coast. Captain Edward Prescott, of the *Sarah Artch*, had allowed his crew to hang Elizabeth in order to end a storm, which they believed her to have caused,

Exactly how Washington knew the particulars of the affair is unknown and although he had issued the complaint, Washington failed to attend the court session in Maryland, attending his son's baptism instead. Maryland's Governor, Josias Fendall, wrote:

Witnesses examined in Virginia will be of no value here, in this case, for they must be face to face with the party accused or they stand for nothing.

The Maryland court issued a second call for witnesses, but no one appeared and Captain Prescott was released.

1665 – Alice Stephens

During the October session of the General Court, Governor Sir William Berkeley and his council examined an accusation of witchcraft against Alice Stephens. The final judgment of the court is unknown although the court clerk recorded the cryptic notation, "Alice Stephens accused as a witch, but not cleared."

1668 – Unknown woman and her children

On November 24, 1668, a pardon was requested of the General Court at Jamestown for calling an unnamed woman and her children witches.

1671 – Hannah Neal

Edward Cole of Northumberland County alleged that Hannah, the wife of Captain Christopher Neal, was a witch. Cole and Mrs. Neal had been at odds with one another ever since they had both arrived from England on the same ship.

In 1671, Cole began telling his neighbors how Hannah had foretold that he and his family would never prosper in Virginia. Just as she had predicted, Cole's family and servants soon grew sick and several of his cattle died.

Even though he presented depositions to the county justices, Cole determined to prove by his own devices that Hannah was a witch who had cursed his family. He sent for Hannah to visit his bedridden wife, and then nailed a horseshoe over the door of his house. Following the logic that a witch could not enter a dwelling so protected, Cole knew that if she hesitated or refused to enter, he would have sufficient proof of her witchcraft. Hannah surprised everyone, however, by not only passing promptly into the house, but also then praying for the sick woman.

Cole, believing in the power of the horseshoe, apologized for his suspicions and stated that his earlier thoughts were "passionately spoken." He agreed to pay all the court costs involved in the suit.

1675 – Joan (Jane) Jenkins

In June of 1675, a justice of the peace and burgess, Captain William Carver, accused Joan Jenkins of Lower Norfolk County of being familiar with evil spirits and using witchcraft. Accordingly, Joan appeared with her husband, Lazarus, at the county court where Captain Carver made his complaint. Either through the weight of evidence or Captain Carver's influence as a "gentleman" of the county, a special jury of both men and women was impaneled to search the Jenkins' house "according to the 118th chapter of doulton."

Using Michael Dalton's *Country Justice* as it's guide, the jury would have looked for "charmes" or "inchantments" and "pictures of Clay or Waxe (like a man)." If the women of the jury went so far as to search Joan's body, they would have looked for a witch's mark or "place upon their bodie" where a familiar would have sought sustenance.

Presumably, they found nothing for there is no further record of Mrs. Jenkins being bound over for a trial. A revealing side note is the fact that Carver had earlier been involved in a property suit with Joan and Lazarus Jenkins, which possibly led to his accusations.

Captain Carver would meet his end at the gallows the very next year as a supporter of Nathaniel Bacon's ill-fated rebellion against Governor Sir William Berkeley.

1679 – Alice Cartwrite

In January of 1678/9, in Lower Norfolk County, four justices of the peace sat upon an examining court to look into the matter of the death of a member of John Salmon's family.

Salmon maintained that Alice Cartwrite had bewitched his child and caused its death. Such an accusation, if supported by evidence, could lead to the accused being transported to the General Court at Jamestown for trial. If convicted of the use of witchcraft "whereby any person shall be killed," Alice would suffer death.

Whatever evidences were presented to the justices are lost, however, the court fell back onto the use of a test to determine if Alice was truly a witch:

Upon the petition and complaint of Jno. Sammon (sic) against Alice the wife of Thomas Cartwrite concerning the death of a child of the said Sammon who it is supposed was bewitched, it is ordered that the Sheriff do forthwith summon an able jury of women to attend the court tomorrow and search the said Alice according to the direction of the court.

The next day, January 16, a jury of women was formed to examine Alice. There is no record of what the court's precise directions might have been to search her, however, the accepted practice was for the accused to be taken into a separate room, where a private and meticulous physical examination could be made. As outlined by several noted authorities, the jury of women would be searching for witch's marks.

Regardless of how the actual examination took place, the jury led by the forewoman, Mary Chichester, delivered their findings to the justices:

In the diff beetween Jno Salmon plantiff agt Alice the wife of Thomas Cartwrite defendt a Jury of women... being Impaneled did in open Court upon their oaths declare that they having delegently Searched the body of the sd Alice & cann find noe Suspitious marks whereby they can Judge her to be a witch butt onley what may and Is usuall on women, It is therefore the Judgment of the Court and ordered that shee bee acquitted and her husbands bond given for her appearance to bee given up.

1694 – Phyllis Money
In 1694, William Earle of Westmoreland County accused Phyllis Money of casting spells and teaching witchcraft. On November 1, he claimed before the

county court that Phyllis had put a spell over a horse owned by her own son-in-law, Henry Dunkin. Earle also added that Phyllis had instructed John Dunkin in how to be a wizard and her daughter on how to be a witch. The accusations were unproven and Phyllis sued for damages, but received nothing.

1695 – Elizabeth Dunkin

Very possibly related to the accusations in Westmoreland County, just the year before, Elizabeth Dunkin was accused by Henry Dunkin of being regularly suckled by the Devil. The charges were not proven and Elizabeth sued for 40,000 pounds of tobacco as damages against her reputation. The county justices awarded only 40 pounds.

Considering the parties involved in both the 1694 and 1695 Westmoreland suits and counter-suits, there appears to have been quite a bit of discord between members of the Dunkin family.

1695 – Eleanor Morris and Nell Cane

In 1695, Anne Ball appears to have been beset by witches. She was sure that Eleanor Morris of King and Queen County was a witch and accused her of being a sorceress. Anne told all who would listen, that Mrs. Morris had bewitched her and "had rid her severall days & nights almost to death." She "despaired" for her life and said that she could prove the accusations. She also claimed to have been visited and ridden twice by another woman of the county, Nell Cane.

Perplexed and angry, Eleanor's husband, William Morris, sued Mrs. Ball in the Essex County Court, for slander. In the complaint, William stated that his wife had resided in King and Queen County (previously part of New Kent County) for 30 years, where she had both a good name and reputation. He went on to say that his wife "never was guilty of any conjuration, witchcraft or enchantment, charmes, or sorcery, or any other such act or acts whereby to hurt anybody." According to Morris, Mrs. Ball had acted with "an evil intent and malitious designe to deprive & destroy" Eleanor's reputation.

Twelve bystanders were sworn in as jury members to hear the complaint of slander. Mrs. Ball declared that she was not guilty of any defamation of character, however, she evidently could not prove her public statements as she had so freely professed earlier.

The jury must have felt that Mrs. Ball was a "gossipmonger," because they found in favor of Eleanor and assessed 500 pounds of tobacco as damages for the plaintiff.

1698 – John and Anne Byrd

In 1698, Charles Kinsey and John Potts of Princess Anne County believed that Anne Byrd and her husband, John, had bewitched them. Kinsey claimed that Anne had ridden him from his house to a neighbor's, while Potts claimed she had ridden him along the seashore to his own house.

On July 8, the Byrds brought two separate suits against Kinsey and Potts for "falsely and scandalously" defaming their name and asking for damages of 100 pounds sterling from each of them. The Byrds claimed that, by their loose talk, Kinsey and Potts had "Reported & rendered as if they were witches, or in league with the Devill."

The two defendants admitted their accusations. Potts stated that he "acknowledgeth that to his thoughts, apprehensions or best knowledge they did serve him Soe," while Kinsey declared that he might have dreamed the whole thing. The jury, after hearing the evidence, seemed to have had reservations about the Bryds, for they found for the defendants in both suits.

1697/8, 1698, 1705/6, 1706 – Grace Sherwood

Towards the end of the seventeenth century, a woman named Grace Sherwood lived in Princess Anne County (Lower Norfolk before 1691), who was destined to become the subject of the most involved and well-known witchcraft investigation to occur in colonial Virginia. Her name has survived well into the present day, as does her reputation as "the Virginia Witch."

Grace was the daughter of a carpenter, John White. By 1680, it is known she was married to James Sherwood, a planter. The Sherwoods had at least three sons and resided in Lynnhaven Parish.

Her troubles began in 1697 when Richard Capps began speaking of Grace as witch. No formal accusation was made to the county court but Capps' talk upset the Sherwoods to the extent that they felt the need to take legal action.

On February 4, 1697/8, James and Grace brought suit for defamation against Capps to the sum of 50 pounds sterling. Richard Capps did not appear in court that day to answer the charge and the suit was continued to the next court session. Sometime before the scheduled court day, the two parties apparently worked the matter out between them, as the suit was dismissed by the agreement of all concerned, one month later, on March 3.

Within six months after she settled the matter against Richard Capps, Grace once again found her neighbors speaking of her as a witch. Now John Gisburne, a constable of the county, and his wife, Jane, were spreading the story that Grace had "bewitched their pigs to Death and bewitched their Cotton." At the same time, another woman, Elizabeth Barnes, made an extraordinary declaration. She claimed that Mrs. Sherwood "came to her one night," apparently without waking her husband, Anthony Barnes, who was sleeping beside her, "and rid her and went out the key hole or crack of the door like a black Catt."

To counter these accusations, Grace and her husband brought separate lawsuits for slander against John and Jane Gisburne and Anthony and Elizabeth Barnes on September 10, 1698. The suits claimed that the defendants had "Defamed and abused the said Grace in her good name and reputation," and asked for one hundred pounds sterling from each of the couples. As added weight to their argument, Grace's husband James brought nine witnesses to the court session to testify against the statements made by John Gisburne and Elizabeth Barnes.

A jury of twelve freeholders was formed from the court's bystanders and both cases were heard. Both Constable Gisburne and Mrs. Barnes pleaded not guilty. The witnesses against them were heard, there was a short deliberation, and in each case the jury foreman brought in a simple decision; "Wee of the jury find for the Defendant."

It was not a good day for the Sherwoods. In addition to having lost both suits and receiving nothing in damages, James Sherwood was required to pay the court costs involved in the transportation and attendance of his nine witnesses.

Upon the death of her husband in 1701, Grace Sherwood was left with a small estate valued at only 3000 pounds of tobacco and the growing animosity of her neighbors. Apparently, previous law suits against those who had slandered her as a witch did little to deter the rumors and gossip.

In 1705, Grace seems to have gotten into a brawl with Elizabeth Hill, a neighbor who had called her a witch, and immediately went to court charging assault and battery. The particulars of the fight are not known, but on December 7, 1705, Grace sued Luke Hill and his wife Elizabeth "in an action of Trespass of assault and battery, setting forth how the defendant's wife had assaulted, bruised, maimed and barbarously beaten the plaintiff." Grace asked for fifty pounds sterling in damages.

Through their attorney, Richard Corbitt, the Hills pleaded not guilty. A jury of freeholders was impaneled and sworn to hear the case. After a short deliberation, the jury found in Grace Sherwood's favor but awarded her only twenty shillings, or one pound, as damages.

Although the judgment represented only 1/50th of what Grace asked, Luke Hill and his wife decided that they needed complete vindication. Whether they were reacting in anger or they truly believed that Grace was a witch and a threat to the community, they went forward to prove their accusations and formally instituted a charge of witchcraft against her.

On January 3, 1705/6, the matter came before the justices of Princess Anne County. The complaint stated that Grace had bewitched Elizabeth Hill and petitioned that the justices investigate the "suspicion of witchcraft." Unfortunately, there was not much to investigate as Grace failed to appear in court to answer the charge. The Sheriff was ordered to have Grace present at the next court session.

On February 6 and 7, the court met again, with Grace in attendance. The justices seemingly wished to end the matter and ordered Luke Hill to pay all the fees involved in the complaint, if he continued. Hill persisted and the justices instructed the sheriff to summon a jury of women for the purpose of searching Grace's person for suspicious marks, indicating a pact with the Devil. The case was continued until the next month.

The court next came together on March 7, with nine justices present. The summoned jury of women was sworn and proceeded to "make due inquiry and inspection into all circumstances." As in other cases, this meant that Grace was probably taken into a private room or home where she was stripped and her body searched for incriminating marks. If the justices were truly attempting to end the matter, they received a surprise when the jury delivered their findings:

Wee of the jury have Serchtt Grace Sherwood and found Two things like titts wth Severall other Spotts.

It is interesting to note that the same Elizabeth Barnes who had several years before been involved in a slander suit instigated by Grace, served as the forewoman of the jury.

The justices of Princess Anne County now faced a quandary. They possibly had a real witch on their hands and were unsure of exactly how to proceed. Luke Hill and his complaint were referred to the Governor's Council and Queen's Attorney in Williamsburg:

At a council held at Her Majesties Royall Capitol 28th day of March 1706: Luke Hill by his petition informing the Board that one Grace Sherwood of Princess

Anne County being suspected of witchcraft upon his complaint to that county court that she bewitched the petitioners wife, the court ordered a jury of women to search the said Grace Sherwood, who upon search brought in a verdict against the said Grace, but the court not knowing how to proceed to judgment thereon, the petitioner prays that the attorney General may be directed to prosecute the said Grace for the same.

The Governor's Council ordered that the Queen's Attorney, Stephens Thompson, consider the matter and make a report back the following month. Accordingly, on April 16, Mr. Thompson delivered his opinion:

Upon perusal of the above order of this honorable Board I do conceive and am of the opinion that the charge or accusation is too general that the county court ought to make further examination of the matters of fact and to have proceeded therein pursuant to the directions and powers of County Courts given by the late act of Assembly in criminal cases made and provided and if they thought there was sufficient cause to (according to law) committed her to the General prison of this Colony whereby it would have come regularly before the General Court and whereupon I should have prepared a bill for the Grand jury and if thy found it I should have prosecuted it.

I therefore with humble submission offer and conceive it proper that the said County Court do make further enquiry into the matter, and if they are of opinion there be cause they act according to the above law and I shall be ready to present a Bill and if found proceed thereon.

Upon receipt of the Queen's Attorney's opinion, the justices of Princess Anne County decided to take his advice and continue their examination. Because they felt a "great Cause of Suspicion," they immediately ordered that the sheriff take Grace into custody until she could give a bond for her appearance at the next session of the court. Following the advice of Dalton's *Country Justice* concerning puppets and images, they also instructed the county sheriff and local constable to make a search of "the Sd graces House and all Suspicious places Carefully for all Images and Such like things as may in any way Strengthen the Suspicion."

On June 6 and 7, 1706, Grace stood before the justices of the county and the investigation continued as a criminal suit. The deputy Queen's Attorney of the county, Maximillian Boush, brought several witnesses forward. In due course, they were each sworn and gave evidence against Grace. She offered no excuses and had little to say in her own defense. At this point, it was discovered that although the Sheriff had summoned another jury of women to come forward to search Grace a second time, not one had shown up at the court. Therefore the sheriff was ordered to summon them to appear a second time, not to search Grace, but "To be Dealt with according to the utmost Severity of the Law," because of their contempt. The sheriff was told to summon a third jury to search Grace's person and to have everyone at the next session of the court.

On Friday, July 5, the court convened once again. Unfortunately for the justices, the sheriff could not gather another jury of women together. Doubtful that they would be able to assemble twelve women to carry out an examination, the court decided upon another test. Stating that they were "willing to have all means possible tryed either to acquit her or to Give more Strength to the Suspician that She might be Dealt with as Deserved," the justices ordered the sheriff to try her by ducking or swimming. This ancient test would determine her guilt or innocence by placing her in a body of water to see if she would float.

The justices expressed at least a small bit of concern over Grace's well being. The test was postponed because of "the weather being very Rainy and Bad" and they did not wish to "endanger her health."

Five days later, at 10 o'clock in the morning of Wednesday, July 10, Grace was taken to a pond on the plantation of John Harper. There, she was stripped to her shift and inspected by several women to insure that she was concealing nothing that would affect the test. She was then bound, hand to foot, with a rope around her body. With the help of men in a boat, whose purpose was to "preserve her from Drowning," the sheriff lowered Grace into the pond from a point of land that survives to the present day as "Witchduck Point." The court and bystanders watched carefully to observe whether she floated (guilty) or sank beneath the water's surface (innocent).

Before the assembled gathering, Grace failed the test. She stayed afloat "Contrary to Custom." Being brought ashore, and presumably still wet, Grace was once again searched by five "ancient women," whom the sheriff had managed to gather. After their examination, they declared:

...on Oath that She is not like them nor noe Other woman that they knew of, having two Things like titts on her private parts of a Black Coller being Blacker than the Rest of her Body...

By now the justices were quite ready to pass the whole matter on to the Queen's Attorney in Williamsburg. The court ordered the sheriff to:

... take the Sd Grace Into his Custody and to Commit her body to the Common Gaol of this County there to Secure her by irons, or Otherwise there to Remaine till Such time as he Shall be otherwise Directed in ordr for her coming to the Common Gaole of the country to bee brought to a Future Tryall there.

Here the exact disposition of Grace Sherwood's case falls into dispute and one can only speculate on what actually followed, as the surviving records are silent. Grace could have spent time in the county jail and been released. She may have been whipped or otherwise punished and then released. She may have been, as ordered, sent to the General Court and examined in Williamsburg. There, the Governor's Council may have found her innocent and released her. On the other hand, they may have found her guilty and imprisoned or punished her by some means. Unfortunately, the legal records of the General Court of colonial Virginia were largely destroyed during the Civil War.

Whatever actually happened to her after her imprisonment by the Princess Anne County authorities, she survived. The extant records indicate that Grace survived to be an old woman.

In June of 1714, she received a grant for 145 acres of land, which had belonged to her father, from Lieutenant Governor Alexander Spotswood. Her will was dated 1733, and it was probated in October 1740, leaving her property to her three sons. Thus, the "Virginia Witch" lived for 34 years after her examination.

1706 – Alice Cornick

While Grace Sherwood was undergoing her examination as a witch by the justices of Princess Anne County, Alice Cornick was involved as a witness in a slander suit before the same court. Unfortunately for all concerned in the case, the dispute was between Thomas Ivy, Alice's son from a first marriage, and Joel Cornick, her stepson from a second. Sometime during, or immediately after the proceedings, a neighbor, Thomas Phillips, publicly referred to Alice as "a witch." It is quite possible that his comments were influenced by the recent local events surrounding Grace Sherwood.

Because of his remarks, Thomas Ivy made a formal complaint on behalf of his mother against Phillips during the July session of the court. With the county justices already distracted over the matter of Grace Sherwood, they must have been quite relieved when Phillips appeared at the September session and admitted that he had wrongfully libeled Alice as a witch. He publicly apologized and the justices ordered Phillips to pay the court costs of the suit.

1706-Mary Rookes (North Carolina)

During the summer of 1706, as the legal proceedings involving Grace Sherwood and Alice Cornick were progressing separately in Princess Anne County, it is curious to note that less than 50 miles south, in North Carolina, another woman was being defamed by her neighbors as a witch.

In July of 1706, Mary Rookes, of the Perquimans District of Albemarle, brought suit in the North

Carolina General Court against Thomas Collings and Walter Tanner. Apparently, the two men had made several accusations of witchcraft against Mary. Collings had stated that she was "a Dammed Witch and have bewitched my wife." Tanner also had claimed to have been bewitched and indicated that he could prove it. Mary petitioned the court that their talk had damaged her "Good name, Fame, Credit, and reputation." She asked for 100 pounds sterling from each of the defendants as damages. A separate jury was sworn in each suit and Mary was awarded a total of six shillings.

Perhaps the accusations against Mary Rookes were prompted by the court cases and gossip occurring in nearby Princess Anne County. In 1706, North Carolina was thinly populated and much of Albemarle County's contact with the world was through Southeastern Virginia. The court records indicate, that like Grace Sherwood, Mary had long been thought to be a witch, having brought suit against another neighbor in 1701, who claimed that she had "Haggridden him."

1730 – Mary (servant of John Samford)

Possibly the last case of witchcraft seen by a Virginia court occurred in October of 1730, in Richmond County. A white indentured servant, known only as Mary and belonging to John Samford, was committed to the county jail on the charge of using "Inchantment, Charm, witchcraft, or Conjuration, to tell where Treasure is, or where goods left may be found." On court day, Mary was examined by the county magistrates, and heard several persons speak against her. Apparently, the evidence was sufficient, for the justices ruled that:

It is the opinion of this Court that the said Mary is Guilty of what is laid to her Charge, it is therefore ordered that the Sheriff take her and Carry her to the Common Whipping post, and give her thirty-nine lashes on her bare back well laid on.

It is worthy of mention that under the witchcraft Statute of James I, Mary's crime was considered "petit" witchcraft, punishable by a year in jail and publicly confessing her sins. The Richmond County court seemingly decided to end the matter at once, showing how Virginia justices altered existing law to their community's needs.

Part the Fifth:

Epilogue

Although the court records are far from complete, there seems to be no serious mention of witchcraft before a Virginia court after 1730. The "Age of Enlightenment" appeared to be displacing earlier beliefs. With the repeal of the witchcraft statutes of James I in 1736, Virginians seemed to have been vindicated in the restraint exercised by their courts. The passing of a new law, however, did not mean that the idea of witchcraft had suddenly ceased to exist.

On the first page of the January 20, 1738 edition of the Virginia Gazette, the following letter and story were reprinted from an English newspaper:

London, July 21, 1737
Sir,
I send you enclos'd a very remarkable Letter concerning the late cruel Usage of a poor old Woman in Bedfordshire, who was suspected of being a Witch. You will see by it, that the late Law for Abolishing the Act against Witches has not abolish'd the Credulity of the Country People; but I hope it has made proper Provision for punishing their Barbarity on such Occasions.
I am Sir
Yours, &c. A. B.

Extract of a Letter about the Tryal of a Witch.

SIR,

    The People here are so predjudic'd in the Belief of Witches that you would think yourself in Lapland, was you to hear their ridiculous Stories. There is not a Village in the Neighborhood but has Two or Three. About a Week ago I was present at the Ceremony of Ducking a Witch; a particular Account of which, may not perhaps be disagreeable to you.

    An Old Woman of about 60 Years of Age had long lain under an Imputation of Witchcraft; who, being willing (for her own Sake and her Children's) to clear herself, consented to be duck'd; and the Parish Officers promis'd her a Guinea, if she should sink; The Place appointed for the Operation, was in the River Oust, by a Mill; there were, I believe, 500 Spectators; About 11 o'Clock in the Forenoon, the Woman came, and was tied up in a wet Sheet, all but her Face and Hands; her Toes were tied close together, as were also her Thumbs, and her Hands tied to the small of her Legs; They fasten'd a Rope about her Middle, and then pull'd off her Cap to search for Pins, for their Notion is, if they have but one Pin about 'em, they won't sink.

    When all Preliminaries were settled, she was thrown in; but, unhappily for the poor Creature, she floated, tho' her Head was all the while under Water; Upon this there was a confus'd Cry, A Witch! A Witch! Hang her! Drown her! She was in the Water about one Minute and a Half, and was then taken out half drown'd; when she had recovered Breath, the Experiment was repeated twice more, but with the same Success, for she floated each Time; which was a plain Demonstration of Guilt to the ignorant Multitude; For notwithstanding the poor Creature was laid upon the

Grass, speechless, and almost dead, they were so far from shewing her any Pity or Compassion, that they strove who should be the most forward in loading her with Reproaches, Such is the dire Effect of popular Predjudice! As for my Part, I stood against the Torrent, and when I had cut the Strings which tied her, had her carried back to the Mill, and endeavored to convince the People of the Uncertainty of the Experiment, and offer'd to lay Five to One, that any Woman of her Age, so tied up in a loose Sheet, would float, but all to no Purpose, for I was very near being mobb'd. Some Time after, the Woman came out; and one of the Company happen'd to mention another Experiment to try a Witch, which was to weigh her against the Church Bible; for a Witch it seems, could not outweigh it. I immediately seconded that Motion (as thinking it might be of Service to the poor Woman) and made use of an Argument, which (tho' as weak as King Jame's for their not sinking) had some Weight with the People; for I told them, if she was a Witch, she certainly dealt with the Devil; and as the Bible was undoubtedly the Word of God, it must weigh more than all the Works of the Devil. This seem'd reasonable to several; and those that did not think it so, could not answer it; At last, the Question was carried, and she was weighed against the Bible; which weighing about twelve Pounds, she outweighed it. This convinc'd some, and stagger'd others; but some who believ'd thro' thick and thin, went away fully assured, that she was a Witch, and endeavored to inculcate that Belief into all others.

Hopefully, by this time, most Virginians would shake their heads in amazement at such nonsense.

Notes on sources and documents of Colonial Virginia.

In order to learn about the cases of witchcraft that appeared in Virginia courts, it is not only necessary to review the very scant amount of secondary sources available, but also to examine the existing original documents and court records of the period.

During the seventeenth and early eighteenth centuries, Virginia's Court records, whether for a specific county or for the General Court, were generally maintained by the clerk of that court. Some clerks were diligent and maintained fine records, safeguarding them over the years. Some were less conscientious, keeping their records at their own homes in trunks or boxes that were left to mold and mildew, as they grew older and less likely to be needed. As Virginia grew, larger counties were divided into smaller ones. The American Revolution and especially the Civil War disrupted courts, and records were moved, hidden, misplaced, or lost to fire or vandalism. By the late nineteenth century when historic preservation became important to many Virginians, there were large gaps in the surviving records.

In attempting to examine and transcribe the remaining court documents, one is faced with the challenge of deciphering the handwriting, spelling, and varieties of abbreviations of numerous clerks over the years.

Court records of the colonial period were not the verbatim documents prepared by court recorders and stenographers of today. Generally, clerks would make notes that would later (sometimes, much later) be entered, possibly with additional information or margin notes, into bound record books. These became the official court records.

Depending on the clerk, you may find excellent and easy-tò-read handwriting, or a barely discernable scrawl that can be extremely frustrating. Many court clerks practiced their own versions of shorthand and abbreviations, in which they attempted to condense lengthy legal documents and save time.

Adding to this frustration, clerks commonly spelled many words and names as they sounded. This could lead to several spellings (or misspellings) of the same person's name, sometimes within the same document. During research, this can cloud the issue of exactly who is involved in a case.

Finally, even the exact dates of certain records can be difficult to determine. Before 1752, England and her North American colonies used the Gregorian calendar. Besides being several days behind much of the rest of the world (eleven days in 1752), the first day of the year was not considered to be January 1 but March 25, the Feast of the Annunciation. Therefore, a typical year would run from March 25 to the following March 24. What might be 1696 in England and Virginia was 1697 in Germany or France.

In an attempt to co-exist with the rest of the world, English dates were written using both the "old style" and "new style." For example, from January 1 until March 24, a date would be written 1696/7, meaning the event occurred in the civil year (March 25-March 24) of 1696, but in the calendar year (January 1- December 31) of 1697.

It was confusing even then.

Appendix 1

The Witchcraft Act of 1604

The Witchcraft Statute of King James I was passed in June of 1604 and dramatically changed the law regarding witchcraft in Great Britain and Virginia.

An Acte against conjuration Witchcrafte and dealinge with evill and wicked Spirits.

BE it enacted by the King our Sovraigne Lorde the Lordes Spirituall and Temporall and the Comons in this p'sent Parliament assembled, and by the authoritie of the same, That the Statute made in the fifth yeere of the Raigne of our late Sov'aigne Ladie of the most famous and happy memorie Queene Eliza-beth, intituled An Acte againste Conjurations In-chantments and witchcraftes, be from the Feaste of St. Michaell the Archangell nexte cominge, for and con-cerninge all Offences to be committed after the same Feaste, utterlie repealed.

AND for the better restrayning of saide Of-fenses, and more severe punishinge the same, be it further enacted by the authoritie aforesaide, That if any pson or persons after the saide Feaste of Saint Michaell the Archangell next comeing, shall use prac-tise or exercsise any Invocation or Conjuration of any evill and spirit, or shall consult covenant with enter-taine employ feede or rewarde any evill and wicked Spirit to or for any intent or purpose; or take any dead man woman or child out of his her or theire grave or any other place where the dead body resteth, or the skin, bone or any other parte of any dead person, to be imployed or used in any manner of Witchecrafte, Sor-

cerie, Charme or Inchantment; or shall use practise or exercise any Witchcrafte Sorcerie, Charme or Incantment wherebie any pson shall be killed destroyed wasted consumed pined or lamed in his or her bodie, or any parte therof ; then that everie such Offendor or Offendors theire Ayders Abettors and Counsellors, being of the saide Offences dulie and lawfullie convicted and attainted, shall suffer pains of deathe as a Felon or Felons, and shall loose the priviledge and benefit of Cleargie and Sanctuarie.

AND FURTHER, to the intent that all manner of practise use or exercise of declaring by Witchcrafte, Inchantment Charme or Sorcerie should be from henceforth utterlie avoyded abolished and taken away, Be it enacted by the authorite of this p'sent Parliament, that if any pson or psons shall from and after the saide Feaste of Saint Michaell the Archangell next cominge, take upon him or them by Witchcrafte Inchantment Charme or Sorcerie to tell or declare in what place any treasure of Golde or silver should or had in the earth or other secret places, or where Goodes or Thinges loste or stollen should be founde or become; or to the intent to Pvoke any person to unlawfull love, or wherebie any Cattell or Goods of any pson shall be destroyed wasted or impaired, or to hurte or destroy any Pson in his bodie, although the same be not effected and done: that then all and everie such pson or psons so offendinge, and beinge therof lawfullie convicted, shall for the said Offence suffer Imprisonment by the space of one whole yeere, without baile or maineprise, and once in everie quarter of the saide yeere, shall in some Markett Towne, upon the Markett Day, or at such tyme as any Faire shalbe kept there, stande openlie upon the Pillorie by the space of six houres, and there shall openlie confesse his or her error and offence ; And if any pson or psons beinge once convicted of the same offences as is aforesaide, doe eftsones ppetrate and comit the like offence, that then everie such Offender, beinge of the saide offences the second tyme lawfullie and duelie convicted and attainted as is aforesaide, shall suffer paines of deathe as a Felon or Felons, and shall loose the benefitt and priviledge of Clergie and Sanctuarie: Saving to the wife of such person as shall offend in any thinge contrarie to this Acte ; her title of dower; and also to the heire and successor of everie such person his or theire titles of Inheritance Succession and other Rights, as though no such Attaindor or the Ancestor or Predecessor had been made; Provided alwaies that if the offender in any cases aforesaide shall happen to be a Peere of this Realme, then his Triall therein is to be had by his Peeres, as it is used in cases of Felonie or Treason and not otherwise.

Appendix 2

A Brief Chronology of
Witchcraft in England and Scotland

Belief in witchcraft in colonial Virginia did not exist in a vacuum. The following list is a brief time-line of what was occurring in England and Scotland in the sixteenth, seventeenth, and eighteenth centuries. The listing is by no means complete and only major witchcraft examinations are mentioned. Between 1590 and 1700, over 5% of all the cases heard in English county courts involved some mention of witchcraft. In the Home Circuit around London, the figure was as high as 13%. It is important to observe that many of the settlers arriving in Virginia throughout the seventeenth and early eighteenth centuries would have carried with them memories of these events.

1542
Statute of Henry VIII against Witchcraft is enacted.

1547
Witchcraft Statute of 1542 is repealed.

1563
Statute of Queen Elizabeth against witchcraft is enacted. Witchcraft is recognized as a crime of the highest magnitude.

1566
Witchcraft trials occur in Chelmsford.

1579

Witchcraft trials occur at Windsor.

1584

Reginald Scot publishes the *Discovery of Witchcraft*.

1589

A series of storms prevents King James VI of Scotland, from meeting his intended bride. Witchcraft is suspected. Witch trials occur in Chelmsford.

1590

Trials of the "North Berwick witches" occur in Edinburgh. King James VI participates in the examinations.

1593

Witchcraft trials occur in Huntingdon.

1595

Witchcraft trials occur in Braynford and Barnett.

1596

Witchcraft trials occur in Edinburgh.

1597

King James VI publishes his treatise on witchcraft, *Demonologie*.

1598

Witchcraft trials occur in Aberdeen.

1603

The author of *Demonologie*, James VI of Scotland, becomes James I of England. Copies of Reginald Scot's book are ordered burned.

1604
Witchcraft Statutes of King James I enacted.

1605
Witchcraft trial occurs in Abingdon.

1612
Witchcraft trials occur in Lancashire.

1619
Witchcraft trials occur in Lincoln.

1621
Witchcraft trials occur in Inverkiething.

1622
Witchcraft trials occur in Glasgow.

1624
Witchcraft trials occur in Bedford.

1630
Witchcraft trials occur in Lancaster and Kent.

1645
Matthew Hopkins, the self-proclaimed "Witch finder-General," becomes active. Witchcraft trials occur in Norfolk and Chelmsford.

1647
Discovery of Witches by Matthew Hopkins is published.

1649

Witchcraft trials occur at Newcastle and St. Albans.

1652

Witchcraft trials occur at Durham, Maidstone and Worcester.

1658

Witchcraft trials occur in Edinburgh.

1664

Witchcraft trials occur at Bury St. Edmonds.

1678

Witchcraft trials occur at Prestonpans.

1682

Witchcraft trials occur in Exeter.

1712

The last official conviction for witchcraft in England occurs.

1722

The last execution for witchcraft in Scotland occurs.

1736

Witchcraft Act of 1604 is repealed and replaced by the Act of 1736. It remains in force until 1951.

Appendix 3

Virginia counties involved with witchcraft accusations, examinations, and related slander suits, 1626-1730.

These are the known cases extracted from surviving records. As General Court cases would generally originate in a county court, both courts may be included in a single examination. Many of the instances of alleged witchcraft are backgrounds to slander suits.

The Governor and/or Governor's Council at Jamestown and later Williamsburg heard the following cases:

Admiralty Court at Jamestown
1654: Investigation into death of Katherine Grady

General Court at Jamestown
1626: Joan Wright
1641: Mrs. George Barker
1657: Barbara Wingbrough
1665: Alice Stephens
1668: Unknown woman and her child
General Court at Williamsburg
1706: Grace Sherwood (It is unclear whether
        the case was actually heard.)

Justices of the Peace of the various counties heard the following cases:

Essex County/King and Queen County
1695: Eleanor Morris and Nell Cane

Lower Norfolk County
1659: Mistress Robinson
1675: Joan Jenkins
1678/9: Alice Cartwrite

Northumberland County
1656: William Harding
1671: Hannah Neal

Princess Anne County
1697/8: Grace Sherwood
1698: John and Anne Byrd
1698: Grace Sherwood
1705/6, 1706: Grace Sherwood
1706: Alice Cornick

Richmond County
1730: Mary (indentured servant of John
    Samford)

Surry County
1626: Joan Wright

Westmoreland County
1694: Phyllis Money
1695: Elizabeth Dunkin

BIBLIOGRAPHY

Booth, Shirley Smith. *The Witches of Early America.* New York: Hastings House, 1975.

Bryson, William Hamilton. *Census of Law Books in Colonial Virginia.* Charlottesville: University Press of Virginia, 1978.

Coleman, Elizabeth Dabney. "The Witchcraft Delusion Rejected." *Virginia Cavalcade*, Vol. VI, No. 1, Summer 1956.

Criminal Proceedings in Colonial Virginia: Richmond County 1710/11 to 1754. Ed Peter Charles Hoffer and William B. Scott, Athens: University of Georgia Press, 1984.

Dalton, Michael. *The Countrey Justice.* London, 1622.

Davies, Owen. *Witchcraft, Magic and Culture 1736-1951.* Manchester, England: Manchester University Press, 1999.

Davis, Richard Beale. "The Devil in Virginia in the Seventeenth Century." *The Virginia Magazine of History and Biography*, Vol. 65, No. 2, April 1957.

Durston, Gregory. *Witchcraft And Witch Trials: A History of English Witchcraft and its Legal Perspectives, 1542 to 1736.* Chichester, England: Barry Rose Law Publishers, 2000.

Gibson, Marion. *Reading Witchcraft: Stories of early English witches*. New York: Routledge, 1999.

Glanville, Joseph. *Saducismus Triumphatus*. London: S. Lownds, 1688.

Guiley, Rosemary. *The Encyclopedia of Witches and Witchcraft*. 2nd Ed. New York: Checkmark Books, 1999.

Hornbook of Virginia History. Ed. Emily J. Salmon and Edward D.C. Campbell, Jr., 4th Edition. Richmond: Library of Virginia, 1994.

Jacob, Giles. *A New Law Dictionary*. 5th Edition. London: Henry Lintot, 1744.

James VI and I. *Daemonologie*. Edinburgh: 1597. London: 1616.

Karlsen, Carol F. *The Devil in the Shape of a Woman: Witchcraft in Colonial New England*. New York: W.W. Norton & Co., 1987.

Klaits, Joseph. *Servants of Satan: The Age of the Witch Hunts*. Bloomington: Indiana University Press, 1985.

Linebaugh, Peter, and Marcus Rediker. *The Many-Headed Hydra: Sailors, Slaves, Commoners, and the Hidden History of the Revolutionary Atlantic*. Boston: Beacon Press, 2000.

Mackay, Charles. *Extraordinary Popular Delusions and the Madness of Crowds*. 1841. Reprint, New York: Harmony Books, 1980.

Mather, Cotton. *The Wonders of the Invisible World*. 1692. Reprint, New York: Dorset Press, 1991.

Minutes of the Council and General Court of Colonial Virginia 1622-1632, 1670-1676. Ed. H. R. McIlwaine, 2nd Edition. Richmond: Virginia State Library, 1979.

Morton, Richard L. *Colonial Virginia: Vol. II Westward Expansion and Prelude to Revolution*. Chapel Hill: University of North Carolina Press, 1960.

Narratives of the Witchcraft Cases, 1648-1706. Ed. George L. Burr. New York: Charles Scribner & Sons, 1914. Reprint, New York: Barnes and Noble, 1975.

North Carolina Higher-Court Records 1702-1708. Ed. William S. Price, Jr. 2nd Series, Vol. IV. Raleigh: North Carolina State University Print Shop, 1974.

Rankin, Hugh F. *Criminal Trial Proceedings in the General Court of Colonial Virginia*. Williamsburg, Va.: Colonial Williamsburg Foundation, 1965.

Salgado, Gamini. *The Elizabethan Underworld*. Gloucestershire: Alan Sutton Publishing Ltd., 1992.

Scot, Reginald. *The Discoverie of Witchcraft*. 1584. Reprint, New York; Dover Publications, 1972.

Sharpe, James. *Instruments of Darkness: Witchcraft in England 1550-1750*. London: Hamish Hamilton Ltd., 1996.

Turner, Florence Kimberly. *Gateway to the World: A History of Princess Anne County, Virginia, 1607-1824*. Easley, South Carolina: Southern Historical Press, Inc., 1984.

Webb, George. *The Office and Authority of A Justice of Peace*. Williamsburg, Va.: William Parks, 1736.

Webster, John. *The Displaying of Supposed Witchcraft*. London: JM, 1677.

Wedeck, Harry, E. *A Treasury of Witchcraft*. New York: Gramercy Books, 1961.

Williams, Selma R. *Riding the Nightmare: Women & Witchcraft from the Old World to Colonial Salem*. New York: Harper Perennial, 1978.

Whitaker, Alexander. *Good Newes from Virginia*. 1613. Reprint: Scholars' Facsimiles & Reprints.